Kisses for Daddy

Frances Watts & David Legge

LITTLE HARE

www.littleharebooks.com

To Nell,
and Frances Watts
—DL

Little Hare Books
8/21 Mary Street, Surry Hills
NSW 2010 AUSTRALIA

www.littleharebooks.com

Text copyright © Frances Watts 2005
Illustrations copyright © David Legge 2005

First published in Australia in 2005
First US edition 2008
Reprinted 2008
Reprinted 2009
Reprinted 2010

For children.
ISBN 9781921714016

Designed by Serious Business
Produced through Phoenix Offset
Printed in Shenzhen, Guangdong Province, China in March 2010

7 6 5 4

This product conforms to CPSIA 2008

Baby Bear was grumbly. He didn't want to go to bed.
He didn't want his bath, and he didn't want to
kiss his mom and dad goodnight.

"Come on, grumbly bear," said his dad. "A big bear kiss for Mom, a big bear kiss for Dad, then bath and bed."

"No," said Baby Bear. But he padded slowly over to Mom and gave her a big kiss anyway.

"Now what about a big bear kiss for me?" said Dad.

"No!" said Baby Bear. "No kiss for Daddy."

"Oh," said Daddy, picking up Baby Bear and lifting him high. "Well, how about a giraffe kiss instead?"

"Baby giraffes give their daddies long,
tall kisses, like this…"

"No!" said Baby Bear.
"No giraffe kiss for Daddy."

"Oh dear," said Daddy, carrying
Baby Bear up the stairs.
"How about a koala
kiss instead?"

"Baby koalas give their daddies cuddly, clingy kisses, like this…"

"No!" said Baby Bear. "No koala kiss for Daddy!"

"Too bad," said Daddy, as he ran the bath.
"How about a crocodile kiss instead?"

"Baby crocodiles give their daddies snappy, watery kisses, like this…"

"No!" said Baby Bear.
"No crocodile kiss for Daddy!"

"Maybe that's just as well," said Daddy, as he rubbed them both dry. "How about a bat kiss instead? Baby bats give their daddies upside down kisses, like this..."

"No!" said Baby Bear.
"No bat kiss for Daddy!"

"That's a shame," said Daddy, as he gave Baby Bear
his toothbrush. "How about a tiger kiss instead?
Baby tigers give their daddies stripy,
growly kisses, like this..."

"No!" growled Baby Bear.
"No tiger kiss for Daddy!"

"Never mind," said Daddy, as he helped Baby Bear with his pyjamas. "How about a monkey kiss instead?"

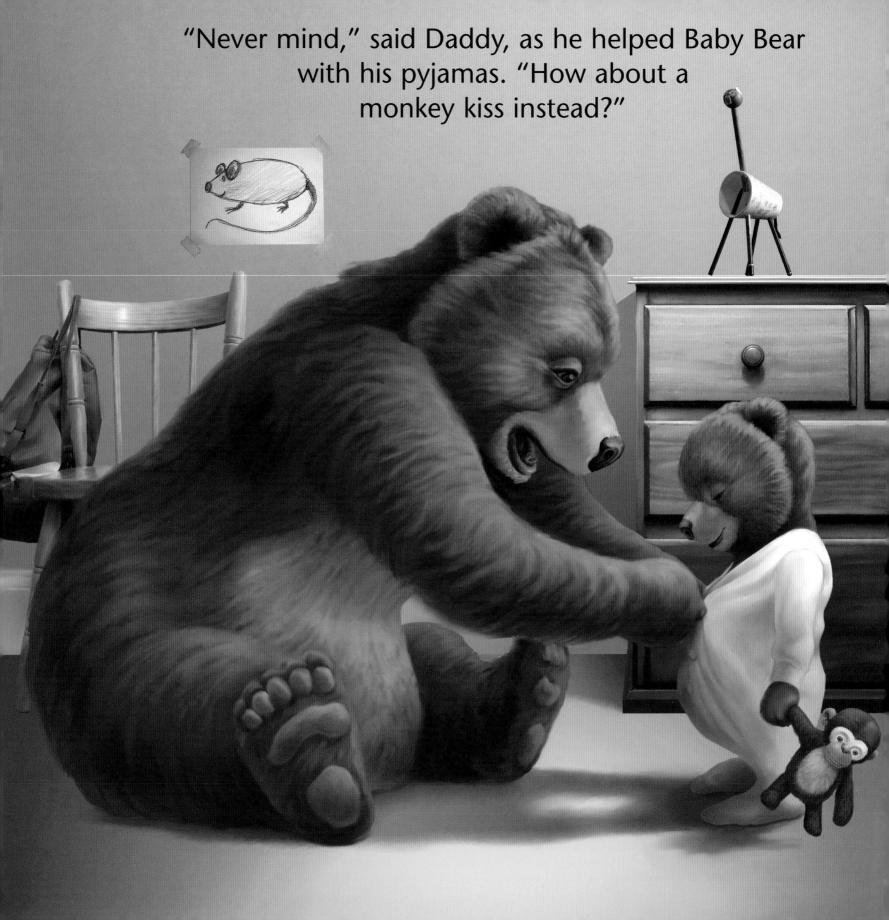

"Baby monkeys give their daddies jumpy, wriggly kisses, like this…"

"No!" giggled Baby Bear. "No monkey kiss for Daddy!"

"What a pity," said Daddy, as he pulled the blanket up to Baby Bear's chin. "How about a mouse kiss instead?"

"Baby mice give their daddies tiny, whiskery kisses."

"No!" squeaked Baby Bear. "No mouse kiss for Daddy!"

Daddy Bear shook his head sadly. "No kisses for Daddy at all, then?" He sighed and started to walk away.

"Daddy!" cried Baby Bear.

"Yes?" said Daddy Bear.

"I do have something for you."
"What is it, Baby Bear?"
asked his dad.

"A big bear kiss—and a big bear hug, too!'